Nancy Drew
and the Clue Crew

#2

Scream for Ice Cream

By Carolyn Keene

Illustrated by Macky Pamintuan

Aladdin Paperbacks
New York London Toronto Sydney

❧ ALADDIN PAPERBACKS

An imprint of Simon & Schuster Children's Publishing Division

1230 Avenue of the Americas, New York, NY 10020

Text copyright © 2006 by Simon & Schuster, Inc.

Illustrations copyright © 2006 by Macky Pamintuan

All rights reserved, including the right of reproduction in whole or in part in any form.

ALADDIN PAPERBACKS, NANCY DREW AND THE CLUE CREW, and colophon are trademarks of Simon & Schuster, Inc.

NANCY DREW is a registered trademark of Simon & Schuster, Inc.

Designed by Lisa Vega

The text of this book was set in ITC Stone Informal.

Manufactured in the United States of America

First Aladdin Paperbacks edition June 2006

10 9 8 7 6

Library of Congress Control Number 2005935598

ISBN-13: 978-1-4169-1253-8

ISBN-10: 1-4169-1253-3

13693
ER
Kee

CONTENTS

CHAPTER ONE

What's the Scoop?

"Can we taste the ice cream now?" Bess Marvin asked.

George Fayne rolled two doubled-up coffee cans on top of the picnic table. The middle can was filled with very cold milk, sugar, vanilla, and blueberries. "I told you a gazillion times, Bess," she said. "Not until it's ready!"

"Unless you want mushy ice cream," eight-year-old Nancy Drew said with a giggle.

Bess and George were Nancy's two best friends. They were cousins, too, but as different as strawberry and fudge ripple ice cream. George was really into computers. Bess could fix or build anything—like the homemade ice-cream maker

1

George found instructions for on the Web.

Nancy had been counting the days until Saturday. That's when the new Jim and Barry's Ice Cream Factory would open on River Street. It was also the day of the Jim and Barry's ice-cream flavor contest. Whoever came up with the best flavor would win a special silver ticket. The ticket would allow the winner to come into the factory any time for a free pint of ice cream!

The thought of Jim and Barry's ice cream always made the girls' mouths water. They had neat flavors like Squirrel Nut Crunch, Gorilla Vanilla, and Cookie Crumble!

For the contest, Nancy, Bess, and George came up with a flavor called Clue-berry. It was vanilla ice cream loaded with blueberries and a secret surprise—like a big juicy strawberry on the bottom.

"The best part," Nancy said, "is the clues on each container leading to the surprise!"

"It's like a mystery in every pint!" George declared.

"And everybody knows we *love* mysteries!" Bess exclaimed.

That's because Nancy, Bess, and George were great at solving mysteries. They had even started their own detective club called the Clue Crew. Their detective headquarters were in Nancy's room. They carefully kept their clues in Nancy's desk drawer. George wrote their detective files on Nancy's computer.

"Can we taste it now?" Bess asked, twirling a lock of her blond hair around her finger.

"Not until it's ready!" Nancy and George said together.

Just then the sound of bells filled the air. Nancy would know that sound anywhere—it was the jingle of the Mr. Drippy ice-cream truck.

"If you want ice cream so badly, Bess," George said, "why don't you buy some from Mr. Drippy?"

"Mr. Drippy?" Bess answered. She gave a little shudder. "I'd rather buy ice cream from Godzilla!"

"Mr. Drippy *is* Godzilla," Nancy said. "He's the meanest ice-cream man in River Heights. Maybe the world!"

The truck pulled up to the sidewalk. Three kids walked over to it. Mr. Drippy leaned out of the square window on the truck. Without a smile he began to bark, "Fall in line! Heads up! First customer—go!"

The first boy in line wore a baseball cap and a very worried look on his face. "Um," he gulped, "Panda Bar."

Mr. Drippy narrowed his eyes. "No please, no Panda Bar!" he declared. "*Next!*"

A girl in a white T-shirt and red shorts marched up to the window. She threw back her shoulders and shouted, "One chocolate ice-cream pop, please, *sir*! Thank you, *sir*!"

Mr. Drippy nodded as he handed the girl the pop.

"See?" Bess whispered. "Mr. Drippy doesn't give ice cream to anyone who forgets to say please or thank you!"

Nancy saw a boy inside the truck. It was Henderson, Mr. Drippy's son. Henderson was in the fourth grade at River Heights Elementary

4

School. He was also the biggest brat in school!

"Henderson probably never says please or thank you," Nancy said. "And he must get all the ice cream he wants."

"Forget it," George said. "If we win this contest we won't ever have to buy ice cream from Mr. Drippy again."

As the truck pulled away from the curb, Henderson leaned out the window. "What's the matter, girls?" he sneered loudly. "Don't you like ice cream?"

"We don't like you," George muttered under her breath.

"At least Jim and Barry are nice," Bess said.

Nancy brushed a wisp of her reddish blond hair from her forehead. "Guess what? My dad read in a newspaper that Jim and Barry will be at the factory tomorrow," she said. "That's when we're supposed to sign up for the contest!"

"I'll be there too!" a voice said.

Nancy, Bess, and George turned their heads. Deirdre Shannon was walking into the yard. Deirdre was in the girls' third-grade class at school. She usually got whatever she wanted— like her own Web site, called Dishing with Deirdre.

"Hi, Deirdre," Nancy said. "We're making ice cream!"

"What a cowinky-dink!" Deirdre said. She held up a small red notebook. "I'm writing about the contest. So I have to taste everybody's ice cream. It's called research."

George tossed her dark curls as she laughed. "You mean it's called getting to eat a ton of ice cream!" she teased.

"Ha, ha," Deirdre said with a frown.

"Our ice cream isn't ready yet, Deirdre," Nancy said. "But Hannah has a pitcher of lemonade in the kitchen."

Hannah Gruen was the Drews' housekeeper. She had been taking care of Nancy since Nancy's mother died when she was only three years old. Hannah cooked the best vegetable lasagna, baked the best cookies, and gave Nancy the best hugs in the whole world.

"Will Hannah give me one of her famous oatmeal cookies, too?" Deirdre asked, her eyes flashing.

"If you say please!" Nancy said.

"I'm there!" Deirdre said, running toward the house.

"Wow," George said. She stopped rolling to

shake out her hand. "My hand hasn't been this tired since I instant-messaged my pen pal in California for an hour."

"An hour?" Bess cried. "You call that instant?"

Suddenly Nancy heard a rustling noise. She thought it was a squirrel in the hedge until she heard a girl's voice hiss, "Nancy! Bess! George!"

"Who's there?" Nancy hissed back.

A girl slowly stood up behind the hedge. It was their friend Kendra Jackson. Her shiny black hair was tied back in a tight ponytail. She wore a pair of black sunglasses. She looked very mysterious. She looked like a spy!

"Hi, Kendra," Nancy said. "What's—"

"Shhhhh!" Kendra said, putting her index finger to her lips. "I need you to keep a secret . . . a TOP SECRET!"

ChaPTER TWo

Kendra's Secret

"We're good at keeping secrets," Nancy said.

"We're detectives," George said. "Secrets are our business!"

Kendra walked into the yard. She was holding a blue and white picnic cooler by the handle. "I know," she said. "That's why I picked you guys to share my secret with."

Bess bounced up and down on the bench. "I love secrets!" she squealed. "What is it? What is it?"

Kendra placed the cooler on the table. She lifted the lid. Nancy looked inside and saw a white Styrofoam container.

"It's my flavor for the contest,"

Kendra explained. "I made it with my grandfather's old ice-cream maker."

"Why did you bring it here?" Nancy asked.

"I need another opinion," Kendra answered. "My mom and dad love it, but parents always love everything their kids do."

Nancy watched as Kendra pulled the lid off the container. The ice cream inside was dark brown.

"I call it Chock Full of Chocolate," Kendra said. "It has chunks of chocolate inside. Four *kinds* of chocolate."

"Four?" Bess asked.

"I can only think of two," Nancy said.

Kendra laid the container on the table. She

gave the girls each a plastic spoon. "Ready, set, go!" she said.

Nancy stuck her spoon inside the container and into her mouth. She felt the ice cream melt on her tongue. The chocolaty flavors exploded in her mouth like fireworks!

"Well?" Kendra asked. "What do you think?"

Nancy swallowed and said, "Three words: OH MY GOSH!"

George was still chewing on a chocolate chunk when she said, "This ice cream is awesome!"

"It's super-awesome!" Bess said.

Kendra gave a little jump. "Do you think it's a winner?" she asked.

"What's a winner? What's a winner?"

All four girls spun around. Standing a few feet away and holding an oatmeal cookie was Deirdre.

Kendra stared at Deirdre with wide eyes. She turned to her cooler and shut the lid. "I've got to go," she said.

"Wait, Kendra! I know you

told Nancy, Bess, and George something," Deirdre said. She turned to the girls and said, "She did—didn't she?"

"Um," Nancy said.

"Er," George said.

Bess shrugged and said, "Only because we're good at keeping secrets!"

Nancy and George glared at Bess. She was sometimes better at keeping secrets than keeping her mouth shut!

"Since when am I *not* good at keeping secrets?" Deirdre asked Kendra.

"Since you spilled the beans about Marcy Rubin's surprise party," Kendra said. "And the time you told me what I'd be getting from my Surprise Santa at school. . . ."

"Don't forget the time you told everybody my real name," George said.

"Give me a break! Everybody knows your real name is Georgia!" Deirdre said. She turned to Kendra. "Tell me your secret, Kendra. Please? Pretty please? With sugar on top?"

Kendra took a deep breath. Then she said,

"Okay, Deirdre. I invented a flavor for the ice-cream contest."

"Cool! What's in it?" Deirdre asked.

"Can't tell you," Kendra said. "Not that you'd steal it, but you might tell people about it on your Web site."

Deirdre's lower lip jutted out. Her face turned red.

They can't have a fight, Nancy thought. *Kendra and Deirdre are good friends!*

"I know, Deirdre," Nancy said. "Why don't you *promise* Kendra you won't write her recipe on your Web site."

Deirdre turned to Kendra. "I won't write your recipe on my Web site," she said. "Cross my heart and hope to croak—drop an eyeball in my Coke!"

"In that case," Kendra said. She lifted the lid of the cooler and pulled out the ice-cream container. "It's called Chock Full of Chocolate. It has four kinds of chocolate—"

Deirdre wasn't listening. She grabbed a spoon, stuck it into the ice cream, then put it into her mouth. The girls watched as Deirdre's eyes popped wide open. Right away she began licking every drop of ice cream off her spoon.

"I'll take a wild guess and say you like it," George said.

"Are you serious? I totally love it!" Deirdre cried. "Chock Full of Chocolate is the real deal!"

"Remember, Deirdre," Kendra said. "You promised."

"Your secret is safe with me," Deirdre said.

Kendra smiled.

"Good," she said. "Who wants to come to my house and see my grandfather's ice-cream maker? He used to make ice cream on the porch with his own grandpa when he was a kid!"

"They had ice cream in those days?" Deirdre asked. "This I've got to see!"

Nancy, Bess, and George decided not to go. They still had a pint of ice cream to make. The Clue Crew said good-bye to Kendra and Deirdre as the two friends left the Drews' front yard.

"I'm glad they're still friends," Nancy said.

Bess was twisting her hair nervously. "What

if Kendra's ice cream is better than Clue-berry?" she asked.

"There's one way to find out," George said. She lifted the lid off their coffee-can ice-cream maker. The ice cream inside wasn't rock hard, but it was firm enough to taste.

One by one the girls tasted their Clue-berry ice cream.

"It's good!" Nancy said.

"But it's not Chock Full of Chocolate." Bess sighed.

"Maybe we should hide a strawberry *and* a chunk of chocolate on the bottom," George suggested.

"Or maybe we should just hope we win," Nancy said.

"I have an idea, Nancy," Mr. Drew said. "Let's have some of your ice cream for dessert."

It was early evening. Nancy's father was barbecuing in the backyard. Mr. Drew was a lawyer. He liked helping Nancy with her Clue Crew cases. He also liked barbecuing in his favorite stain-splattered red and white checked apron.

"Sorry, Daddy," Nancy said. "Our ice cream is for the contest this Saturday."

Mr. Drew pretended to look hurt.

"But don't worry," Nancy said. "If we win the contest, we'll have a different Jim and Barry ice cream every week!"

Hannah walked over carrying a bowl of fruit salad with walnuts. Nancy's Labrador retriever puppy, Chocolate Chip, jumped after her.

"What about my desserts?" Hannah asked. "Those guys will put me out of business!"

Nancy wrapped her arms around Hannah's waist and gave her a big hug. "That will never happen, Hannah," she said. "Your desserts rock!"

The cordless phone on the patio table rang. Nancy ran to answer it. "Hello?" she asked.

"Sh-she did it!" Kendra's voice stammered. "I told you she'd do it—and she did it!"

"Who did what, Kendra?" Nancy asked.

"Deirdre!" Kendra said. "She broke her promise!"

ChaPTER ThReE

Backpack Attack

"No way!" Nancy gasped. "Did Deirdre write your secret recipe on her Web site?"

"No," Kendra answered. "But she did write that I had a winning recipe."

"What's wrong with that?" Nancy asked.

"Don't you see?" Kendra asked. "Now all the kids in the conest will want to steal my secret recipe!"

Nancy shook her head, even though she knew Kendra couldn't see her do it over the phone. "They can't do that unless you *tell* them your recipe," she said. "Besides, most of the kids we know are honest."

"Yeah," Kendra snorted. "Until they want to win free ice cream!"

Click!

Kendra had hung up. But Nancy wasn't worried. Tomorrow they would all sign up for the contest. It would be so exciting that Kendra would forget about Deirdre's Web site.

Nancy reached down to scratch Chocolate Chip behind her floppy little ears. "And may the best ice cream win!" she declared.

"There it is," Bess said, pointing. "Is that the most awesome building you ever saw in your whole life?"

"And just think," Nancy said. "It's filled with the yummiest ice cream in the whole wide world!"

It was Thursday morning. Hannah had driven Nancy, Bess, and George to the Jim and Barry's Ice Cream Factory. A huge crowd of kids

18

stood in front of the factory, all set to sign up for the ice-cream flavor contest.

Nancy could see a stage set up in front of the factory. Purple, yellow, and white balloons swept over the stage in an arch.

"If this is just for the sign-up," Nancy said, "I can't wait to see what they do for the contest!"

"I'm going down the street to buy some fruits and vegetables," Hannah said. "Stay here and stay together."

Nancy, Bess, and George nodded. The friends all had the same rules. They could walk or ride their bikes five blocks from their houses as long as they were together. Anywhere farther than that, they had to be driven by a parent or Hannah.

"And if you get any free ice-cream samples," Hannah said with a wink, "save one for me!"

Nancy hugged Hannah good-bye. Then the three excited friends joined the crowd. Music blared from loudspeakers as kids from the River Heights Dance School tapped across the stage in ice-cream cone costumes. Nancy saw their friend Nadine Nardo dancing with the group.

Nadine wanted to be an actress and loved being on stage. But today she was frowning as her ice-cream hat began tipping over her face.

Mayor Strong stood on the side of the stage. He was smiling and holding a folded piece of paper in his hand.

Probably his speech, Nancy thought. *Mayor Strong loves making speeches.*

Nadine's hat fell off as she took a bow. Then the dancers tapped off the stage.

"Wasn't that great?" Mayor Strong asked as he walked onto the stage. He put on a pair of glasses, unfolded his speech, and began to read. "You know, when I was a kid—"

Nancy heard George groan under her breath. Mayor Strong always talked about being a kid.

"—we had only one ice-cream parlor, and it sold only two flavors!" Mayor Strong said. "Can you imagine that, kids?"

"Is he kidding?" a voice muttered. "I'd do a headstand on a pyramid for just *one* flavor."

Nancy turned around. Standing behind them was a boy from their class named Kevin Garcia.

Kevin's parents owned the Mean Bean Health Food Store on River Street. Kevin wasn't allowed to eat sweets, so he always mooched snacks from everybody's lunchboxes.

"What are you doing here, Kevin?" Nancy asked. "You're not allowed to eat ice cream."

"I heard Jim and Barry are giving away free samples of ice cream," Kevin said. He leaned closer to the girls and whispered, "Got any candy on you?"

"No," Nancy said.

"Hey," Kevin said. "Is it true that Kendra has a winning recipe for the contest?"

Bess and George raised their eyebrows at Nancy. She had told them that morning about Deirdre and her Web site.

"Um . . . maybe," Nancy blurted.

"Got any gum?" Kevin asked.

"No!" George said. "And don't ask us again!"

Kevin looked disappointed. He turned around and disappeared into the crowd.

"Kevin must have read Deirdre's Web site," Bess said.

Nancy looked for Kendra and found her in the crowd. Everyone near Kendra was pointing at her.

"I guess a *lot* of kids read Deirdre's Web site," Nancy said.

The mayor was still giving his speech. "I even remember riding my shiny red bicycle all the way to the next town for another flavor. But when I got there, they also had only two flavors!"

One or two people in the audience laughed.

"Where are Jim and Barry?" George asked. She stood on her tiptoes to see over the crowd. "I don't see them yet!"

"They're probably scooping out the free samples," Nancy said, rubbing her tummy.

"I hope it's not Marshmallow Martian," Bess said. She stuck her finger in her mouth, pretending to gag.

"Yes, Bess," Nancy said with a smile. "We know how much you hate green ice cream, no matter how good it is!"

A voice snapped, "What's wrong with Marshmallow Martian?"

Nancy, Bess, and George spun around. Standing behind them this time was fourth grader Daisy Dorfer and members of the Jim and Barry Fan Club. Daisy started the club for the summer. They met every week to taste a new Jim and Barry flavor that they picked out at the supermarket.

"Nothing's wrong with it," Bess said with a shrug. "It just makes me—"

"—want more!" Nancy cut in.

"Good," Daisy said. "Because Marshmallow Martian is my favorite flavor!"

Nancy heard Bess gagging under her breath.

"Um," Nancy said, trying to switch the subject. "Are you guys entering the contest?"

Peter Patino from the girls' third-grade class said, "Daisy's dad bought her an electronic ice-cream maker. It has digital controls and everything!"

"Now all we need is a recipe," fourth grader Melissa Rios said. She was wearing dangly ice-cream cone earrings.

Daisy planted her hands on her hips. "We'll

have one, okay?" she said. "And when we do—it'll be the best!"

"The best! The best!" the members chanted.

"It better be the best," Melissa whispered to Nancy. "Because we want to win more than anything!"

A roaring cheer made everyone face the stage.

"It's them!" Daisy swooned. "Jim and Barry!"

Jim and Barry waved to the crowd as they ran onto the stage. Nancy knew it was them from their picture on the ice-cream containers. Jim had copper red hair and wore round wire-rimmed glasses. Barry had a beard and wore a straw hat with a bright purple hatband.

"I scream, you scream, we all scream for ice cream!" Barry shouted.

"How do you like our new factory?" Jim called out. "Pretty cool, huh?"

Cheers filled the air.

"Who here thinks they can make an ice cream that'll rock our worlds?" Barry asked.

Nancy's hand shot up. So did dozens of others.

Jim held up a clipboard. "Well, then step right

up and put your names on the sign-up list!" he boomed.

The crowd began to squeeze into a single line. Deirdre Shannon ran over to Nancy, Bess, and George. She held up a camera and said, "Say Strawberry Cheesecake Ice Cream!"

"How about just cheese?" George asked.

"Cheese!" the three friends said as Deirdre snapped a picture. They knew the picture she was taking was for her Web site.

"Thanks," Deirdre said. "Now I've got to get a picture of Jim and Barry!"

Nancy glanced back. Kendra was lining up too. Daisy was standing right behind her, trying not to be bumped by Kendra's backpack.

I'm sure Kendra's recipe is still a secret, Nancy thought. *How could anyone steal it if it's inside her head?*

Nancy was about to inch her way up the line when she heard a voice yell, "Jim and Barry's flavors stink on ice!"

The girls turned their heads. Standing next to the line was Henderson, the son of Mr. Drippy.

He was holding a sign that read, JIM AND BARRY'S ICE CREAM MAKES ME BARF!

"Jim and Barry's ice cream gave me cooties!" Henderson shouted. "The raisins in the Rum Raisin are really ants! The cherries in the Cherry Vanilla are really squishy eyeballs. Alien eyeballs!"

"That's gross!" Bess said.

"So is Jim and Barry's ice cream!" Henderson said. He cackled meanly. Then he walked away

yelling, "Jim and Barry mix their ice cream with their feet!"

"That's one kid who won't be entering this contest," Nancy said. "He hates Jim and Barry's ice cream!"

The girls finally reached the sign-up list. They wrote their names neatly and clearly.

"We did it!" Bess said, jumping up and down.

"Now all we have to do is bring our Clueberry ice cream to the contest on Saturday!" Nancy said excitedly.

Next the girls picked up their free samples of Rootin' Tootin' Raspberry ice cream. They waited for Hannah as they ate out of little cups with tiny spoons.

"This flavor rocks!" George said.

"And it's not green." Bess sighed with relief.

Nancy was about to take another spoonful when Kendra ran over. Her dark eyes were flashing wildly.

"My s-secret r-r-recipe!" Kendra stammered. "Someone stole it!"

CHAPTER FOUR

Supermarket Surprise!

"How could it be stolen, Kendra?" Nancy asked. "The recipe was inside your head!"

"I wrote it on a piece of paper and brought it today," Kendra explained. "I wanted Jim and Barry to autograph it!"

Kendra held up her backpack. She pointed to the back pocket and said, "It was in that pocket. Now it's gone."

Deirdre ran over with her camera. "Hi, Kendra," she said. "Do you want to pose for my camera?"

Kendra stuck out her tongue and said, "How's that?"

"Not cool." Deirdre shook her head.

"Neither was telling the world I had a winning

recipe," Kendra said. "Now my recipe is stolen and I can't enter the contest!"

"Stolen?" Deirdre gasped. "No way!"

"You can still enter the contest, Kendra," George said. "You do know your recipe by heart, don't you?"

"Big deal," Kendra asked. "The thief who stole my recipe will probably make the same ice cream!"

"What are you going to do?" Bess asked.

"We have to find the robber by Saturday," Kendra said. "*Before* he or she enters the contest."

"We?" Nancy repeated.

"You *are* the Clue Crew, right?" Kendra asked.

"Right," George said. "But Saturday is in two days!"

Nancy felt sorry for Kendra. And she didn't want Kendra and Deirdre to fight. "We'll do it, Kendra," she said. "We'll help you find that creepy recipe thief."

Kendra heaved a sigh of relief. "Thanks, you guys!" she said.

Deirdre pointed her camera at Nancy, Bess, and George. "Smile and say, 'The Clue Crew is on the case!'" she said.

The girls each gave a thumbs-up as Deirdre took the picture.

"Perfect!" Deirdre said as she ran off.

Hannah honked her car horn as she drove up to the curb. Nancy, Bess, and George waved good-bye to Kendra as they climbed into the car.

"I know you can do it," Kendra called as the car pulled away. "The Clue Crew rules!"

When they reached the Drew house, the girls thundered up the stairs to their detective head-quarters. Bess sat on Nancy's bed and bounced a stuffed unicorn on her lap. George sat at Nancy's desk and turned on the computer. Her eyes were glued to the screen as she began a new case file.

"If this mystery is about ice cream," Bess said, "does that make it a cold case?"

"No, Bess," Nancy said. "A cold case is a case that hasn't been solved. My dad told me that while we were watching a mystery show on TV."

"And we *are* going to solve this mystery," George said. "File's up. What do we know so far?"

Nancy paced across her shaggy lavender carpet. "The person who stole Kendra's recipe is probably a kid," she said slowly. "Someone who knew about the recipe and wants to win really badly."

"The Jim and Barry Fan Club wants to win badly," Bess said. "They said so themselves."

"And Daisy Dorfer was standing right behind Kendra in the sign-up line!" Nancy remembered.

"Daisy Dorfer," George said as she typed. "Suspect number one."

Bess tossed the unicorn in the air. "Kevin Garcia asked about Kendra's recipe," she said. "What about him?"

Nancy shook her head. "Why would Kevin enter a contest for something he can't eat?" she asked.

"Especially since his parents would have to sign a permission slip if he won," George added.

Next the girls thought of all the things the thief would need to make Kendra's recipe. First up: chocolate. Lots and lots of chocolate!

"Speaking of ice cream," George said. She

turned around in her chair. "I wonder how our flavor is doing."

"Let's taste it!" Bess said.

"We already tasted it," Nancy said.

George shrugged. "We didn't taste it after it was in the freezer for hours!" she said.

The girls raced out of Nancy's room and ran downstairs into the kitchen. Nancy opened the freezer and pulled out the ice-cream container. As she pulled off the lid—

"Woof!"

Chip jumped up against Nancy. She dropped the whole container on the floor with a *thunk!*

"No!" Nancy cried. Vanilla ice cream and blueberries had spilled onto the floor in big frozen clumps.

The girls stared at Chip lapping up the ice cream.

"At least it wasn't chocolate." George sighed. "Chocolate isn't good for dogs."

Nancy felt awful. If only she had held the container tighter. If only she wasn't such a klutz!

"Now we'll have to make our ice cream all over again," Nancy said. "And that means buying more ingredients."

Hannah came into the kitchen with a mop. "I'd drive you to the supermarket, girls," she said. "But I have a casserole in the oven."

"I'll call my mom," George said. "She goes to the supermarket almost every day."

Louise Fayne owned her own catering company. She planned parties all over River Heights and even provided the food. To Nancy, Mrs. Fayne's van always smelled like coleslaw and pickled tomatoes.

"I'm picking up fruit platters for Mayor Strong's birthday party this Saturday," Mrs. Fayne said as she drove her van. "It's going to be the party of the year!"

Nancy, Bess, and George sat behind Mrs. Fayne. The seat behind them was filled with coleslaw containers.

"Why is Mayor Strong's birthday party the same day as the ice-cream contest?" Bess asked.

"That's how it worked out," Mrs. Fayne said as she pulled the van into the supermarket parking lot.

Once inside the supermarket, Nancy saw lots of other kids. Their baskets and shopping carts were filled with all kinds of foods to make ice cream with.

"I have to go to the deli section," Mrs. Fayne said. "You can pick up your own items as long as you stay together and don't run."

The girls nodded. Shopping on their own always made them feel grown-up!

Mrs. Fayne walked away. Nancy grabbed a red plastic shopping basket, while George unfolded their shopping list. Bess walked to the dairy section for a container of milk. After putting it in the basket, they looked for blueberries.

"Fruit is against the wall," George said. "The healthy stuff is always against the walls."

Bess started to run down the aisle. "Last one there is a rotten watermelon!" she called.

"Bess, wait!" Nancy called. "We're not supposed to run in the supermarket, remember?"

Nancy and George raced after Bess. When they all reached the end of the aisle they sped around the corner.

Wham! The girls slammed right into Kevin Garcia!

Nancy dropped her basket with the container of milk. Luckily the milk didn't open and spill.

But everything tumbled out of Kevin's basket. There was a box of chocolate ice-cream pops, a package of chocolate-dipped ice-cream cones, two cans of chocolate drink, and three jumbo chocolate bars. Nancy stared at Kevin's packages on the floor. Kevin wasn't allowed to eat sweets. What was he doing with all that chocolaty stuff?

"Sorry, you guys," Bess said.

Kevin muttered something under his breath. He picked up his packages and shoved them back into his basket. Then he stood up and quickly walked away.

"Did you see that?" George asked.

"I sure did," Nancy said, nodding. "Kevin's basket was *chock full of chocolate*!"

CHAPTER FIVE

Sticks and Cones

"Kevin would need chocolate to make Kendra's ice-cream flavor," Bess said. "I told you he was a suspect!"

Nancy shook her head. "Kevin is always trying to get his hands on sweets," she said.

Tweeeeeee!!

The shrill sound of a whistle made the girls jump. Nancy whirled around. Daisy and the Jim and Barry Fan Club were standing at the end of the aisle. Daisy was wearing a yellow Jim and Barry Gorilla Vanilla T-shirt and a silver whistle around her neck.

"Okay, group!" Daisy said. "We have our shopping lists. Now let's move out!"

The fan club nodded. Then they spread out in many different directions.

"Daisy is one of our suspects," Nancy whispered. "Let's see what we can find out."

Daisy was wiping her whistle on her T-shirt when the girls walked over.

"Hi, Daisy," Nancy said. "Did you come up with a flavor for the contest?"

"You bet!" Daisy said. "And it's a sure winner!"

"What is it?" Bess asked.

"As if I'm going to tell you," Daisy said. "Only club members can know the top secret recipe."

Daisy swung her whistle as she walked away.

"Only members can know the top secret recipe," George mimicked. "Give me a break!"

"Let's follow the members around," Nancy said in a low voice. "And see what they're buying."

They were about to walk when—

"Girls!" Mrs. Fayne called. "We have to go now."

Nancy grabbed a carton of blueberries on their way to the checkout counter. They couldn't follow Daisy or the club. But they had a great clue. The fan club had a recipe. And it was top secret—just like Kendra's was!

"Now if we can just find out what it is!" Nancy said.

"Is your arm getting tired, George?" Nancy asked. George rolled the coffee can back and forth over the Faynes' doorstep.

"Nah, I'm on a roll!" George joked.

The girls were in the Faynes' front yard making their second batch of ice cream. They didn't want to be near Chip when their ice cream was finished.

"Can I taste it now?" Bess asked. She waved a plastic spoon in the air.

"Don't start that again, Bess," George groaned.

"Hey, Clue Crew!" a voice called.

The girls looked up. Their friend Marcy Rubin was passing by the yard with her five-year-old sister, Cassidy.

"Hi-yeee!" Cassidy called. "Want to see my brand-new sneakers?"

"They're not new, Cassidy," Marcy said. "They used to belong to me."

Cassidy stared down at her red and white sneakers. "No wonder they smell," she said.

Nancy, Bess, and George walked over to Marcy.

"We were just making ice cream for the contest, Marcy," Nancy said.

"How do you have time?" Marcy asked. "Aren't you guys solving the case of Kendra's missing ice-cream recipe?"

Nancy, Bess, and George shared surprised looks.

"Who told you that?" Nancy asked.

"I read it on Deirdre's Web site," Marcy said. "She wrote that the Clue Crew will solve the case for sure. There was even a neat picture of you guys all giving a thumbs-up!"

"Did she give away Kendra's recipe?" Nancy asked.

"Nope," Marcy said.

Nancy sighed with relief. "At least she didn't do that," she said.

"Hey," Marcy said, looking to her side. "Where's Cassidy?"

The girls spun around. Cassidy was sitting on the doorstep eating Clue-berry ice cream from the coffee can!

"Yummy for the tummy!" Cassidy shouted.

"Drop that spoon now, you little pest!" Marcy shouted as she raced over to Cassidy.

"Our second batch of ice cream," George groaned.

"Maybe we aren't meant to enter this contest." Bess sighed.

Nancy smiled as she watched Marcy wrestling the spoon out of her little sister's hand.

"Oh, yes we are," Nancy said. "Cassidy likes it. So maybe Jim and Barry will too!"

"I think Daisy did it, Dad," Nancy said that night. "She was standing right behind Kendra. And she said their new recipe was top secret and a winner!"

Mr. Drew looked up from the newspaper he was reading. He liked reading the paper in his favorite chair every night. "Try not to jump to conclusions, Nancy," he said.

Nancy wrinkled her nose and said, "Jump where?"

"It means don't end your case before you check out everything," Mr. Drew said with a smile. "Things aren't always what they seem to be, you know."

"Okay, Daddy," Nancy said. "But it sure seems like Daisy took Kendra's recipe."

It was still light outside, so Nancy had permission to play in the yard. With Chip at her heels, she skipped to the front door.

"Come on, Chip," Nancy said. "Let's see if you can catch a Frisbee!"

Nancy swung the front door open. As she stepped outside she felt something crunch under her foot. She looked down and gasped. A message had been left on her doorstep. It read, "GIVE UP!"

Nancy looked closer.

The message was written with wooden Popsicle sticks!

ChaPTER Six

Club Flub

"Eww, don't touch them!" Bess warned. "If they're Popsicle sticks—they've been licked!"

It was Friday morning. The Popsicle sticks from the weird message the night before were spread out on Nancy's desk.

"Licked Popsicle sticks usually have ice-cream stains on them," Nancy said. "These don't."

"That makes it even weirder!" George said.

Nancy picked up a stick and flipped it over in her hand. "Each stick has the words Lickety Sticks Company stamped on it," she said. "That must be the place where these Popsicle sticks were made."

"Who would leave such a creepy message?" Bess asked.

"Thanks to Deirdre, everyone knows we're trying to solve Kendra's case," Nancy said. "So the person who stole Kendra's recipe probably wants us to give up."

"But who would have that many Popsicle sticks?" Bess asked.

The girls thought in silence. Suddenly George snapped her fingers and said, "Kevin had a box of Popsicles in his shopping basket."

"A box like that holds only six Popsicles," Nancy said. "A lot more sticks were used to write that message."

"Maybe it's more than one person," Bess said. "Daisy's fan club eats ice cream all the time. And Jim and Barry make Popsicles too."

"I wish we could go to a club meeting," Nancy said. "Then we could find out what kind of ice cream they're making for the contest."

George pointed to a calendar hanging over Nancy's desk. "Today is Friday," she said. "Doesn't the Jim and Barry Fan Club meet every Friday?"

"How can we go to go a meeting if we're not members?" Bess asked.

The girls didn't say a word as they thought. Then Nancy had a brainstorm.

"I know! Let's join the club!" Nancy said.

"I don't want to join that dumb club!" Bess whined. "Daisy is so bossy."

"And we already have a club," George said. "A detective club."

"We'll just be joining to get their top secret recipe," Nancy explained. "We don't have to go to any meetings after that."

The girls knew that Daisy lived on Sparrow Street. George turned on the computer and found Daisy's street on a special Map Search site.

"Only four blocks away," George announced. "We can go there together."

Bess and George already had their bikes and helmets at Nancy's house. Nancy grabbed hers and the three pedaled to Daisy's house.

As the girls rode, the Mr. Drippy truck rambled past them. Henderson stuck his head out the window and shouted, "Ewww! It's the Clue Creeeeew!"

"How does he know we're the Clue Crew?" Bess called from her bike.

"Probably from school," Nancy called back.

"We're famous!" George declared with a smile.

The three girls turned onto Sparrow Street. They parked their bikes against a big tree on the sidewalk. Then they walked up the cobblestone path to Daisy's house.

A teenage boy opened the door after the girls knocked. "You're here for my sister's meeting?" he asked. "So what's the secret password?"

Password? The girls traded worried looks.

"Um . . . cone?" Nancy guessed.

"Sprinkles?" Bess asked.

"Banana split?" George said.

The boy stared at the girls. Then he cracked up laughing. "There is no password!" he said. "You fell for it. I am so gooooood!"

George rolled her eyes as the boy yelled for his sister. "Brothers!" she groaned. "I've got two of them!"

Daisy came running to the door. She looked surprised to see Nancy, Bess, and George.

"Hi, Daisy," Nancy said. "We want to join the Jim and Barry Fan Club!"

"You want to join right before the contest?" Daisy asked. "You don't want to steal our secret recipe, do you?"

"No way!" Nancy said. "We have our own recipe for the contest, remember?"

Daisy folded her arms as she looked from Nancy to Bess to George. "Okay," she said. "But every member has to pass a taste test first."

"You mean taste ice cream?" Bess asked.

"All right!" George cheered. "That's one pop quiz we *want* to take!"

Nancy, Bess, and George followed Daisy into the house. As they walked through the kitchen, Daisy introduced them to her mother. Mrs. Dorfer was on her knees stuffing cans and boxes into a big blue recycling bag. Daisy then led the girls downstairs to the basement. The fan club was sitting cross-legged on the floor. Melissa and Peter waved to the girls. Nancy thought most of the kids looked friendly.

"Peter's T-shirt says Marshmallow Martian," Bess whispered. "Yuck-o!"

"Shhh!" Nancy warned. "We have to love all the flavors or they won't let us join the club."

Daisy walked to a desk near the door. She held up a writing pad and said, "I just wrote our recipe nice and neat for Jim and Barry to read tomorrow."

Nancy, Bess, and George stepped forward.

"Nuh-uh!" Daisy said. She ripped the page off the writing pad. "Not until you join the club."

"Sure," Nancy said. "Let the taste test begin!"

Soon Nancy, Bess, and George were sitting on chairs in the middle of the room. Club members giggled as they tied colorful bandannas over the girls' eyes. Nancy couldn't see but she could hear everyone chatting excitedly. She could even smell something sweet—like ice cream!

"George is first," Daisy said. "Give her the bowl, Melissa."

Nancy heard George's spoon clatter against ceramic. Then she heard a gulp as if George was swallowing.

"Well?" Daisy asked.

"It has a definite nutty taste," George's voice said. "With a touch of caramel . . . and just a hint of—"

"What is it already?" a boy demanded.

"Peanut Brittle Blast!" George said.

The club members applauded.

"Correct," Daisy said. "You can take your blindfold off, George."

Next was Nancy's turn. She felt an ice-cream bar being shoved into her hand. Taking a bite, she began to chew. The ice cream was crunchy, as if it had bits of candy inside.

"I'm pretty sure this is Toffee Coffee," Nancy said.

More applause.

"You guys are good!" Daisy exclaimed.

Nancy whipped off her blindfold. Still eating the ice cream, she turned to George and winked.

"Bess is last," Daisy said. "Give her the ice cream, Melissa."

Melissa smiled as she stepped forward with a bowl. Nancy gasped when she saw the mound of ice cream inside the bowl. It was bright green!

Oh, no! Nancy thought. *It's Marshmallow Martian!*

ChaPTER SEVEN

Candy-Handed

Nancy glanced sideways at George. She was staring at the green ice cream too.

"Um, Daisy," Nancy said. "That flavor is too easy!"

"What are you talking about?" Daisy asked.

"Bess likes hard test questions!" George piped in.

"Since when?" Bess said. She smiled under her blindfold and shouted, "Bring it on!"

Nancy held her breath as Bess took the bowl. Still blindfolded, Bess felt around for the spoon. Carefully she took a spoonful, than stuck it straight into her mouth.

Bess's chin moved up and down. Suddenly her eyebrows flew up above the blindfold. She puffed out her cheeks and spit the ice cream back into the bowl. "Bleeeech!! Marshmallow Martian! Gross! Phooey!"

Bess whipped off her blindfold. She jumped up, leaving the bowl of ice cream on her chair. Nancy and George jumped up too.

"Maybe there was a hair in it!" Nancy said.

The club members stared open-mouthed at Bess. Daisy folded her arms across her chest and said, "We only take members who love *all* of Jim and Barry's ice-cream flavors."

"Yeah," Peter sneered. "Maybe Mr. Drippy has a fan club you can join!"

Nancy stared back at the club members. They didn't look so friendly anymore.

"Er—we have to go," Nancy said quickly.

"We have tons of homework!" George said.

"In July?" Daisy asked.

"It's never too early to start!" Nancy said with a smile. In a flash the girls raced out of the basement room. They said a polite good-bye to Mrs. Dorfer, then raced out of the house to their bikes.

"It's my fault!" Bess wailed. "I blew it!"

Nancy took one last bite of her ice-cream bar. "You were just being honest, Bess," she said. "Besides, we didn't want to join that club anyway."

"Now we'll never find out their secret recipe for the contest," Bess wailed.

"Who says we won't?" George asked.

Nancy and Bess turned to George. She was holding a piece of paper in her hand and grinning from ear to ear.

"Look what I grabbed on the way out," George said. "It's the paper that was underneath the recipe they wrote."

"It's blank!" Bess said.

"Not exactly," George said. She pointed to the

paper. "Check out the scratches on it. Those are the marks the pen made when Daisy wrote the recipe on the top page."

"I get it!" Nancy said. "If we can read the scratches, we can read the recipe."

"How?" Bess asked.

Nancy stuck the Popsicle stick in her pocket. She pulled a pencil out of her waist pack and said, "Watch. It's a trick I learned in a mystery book."

Nancy used the side of the pencil point to lightly draw over the scratches. The words appeared like magic!

"What does it say?" Bess asked.

The girls studied the paper.

"It says . . .

'Oatmeal Cookie and Raisin Crunch Ice Cream,'" Nancy said. "Not Chock Full of Chocolate."

"How do we know it's for real?" George asked. "Maybe they just wrote a fake recipe to trick us."

Nancy carried the Popsicle stick to a trash can in front of the Dorfers' house. On the sidewalk next to the can was a big blue recycling bag—the same bag Mrs. Dorfer was stuffing things into before.

Nancy kneeled down and peered through the clear blue plastic. "Look!" she said, pointing with the Popsicle stick. "This bag is filled with empty raisin containers and oatmeal cookie boxes."

George looked at the list of ingredients on the scratchy paper. "That's what they used to make the ice cream," she said. "I guess the club didn't make Chock Full of Chocolate."

Nancy glanced at the Jim and Barry Popsicle stick in her hand. The words "Lickety Sticks Company" were not stamped on it. "They didn't write the creepy message, either," she said.

The girls took the Jim and Barry Fan Club off

the suspect list. They decided to sit down and come up with more suspects.

"Can we talk over fruit smoothies?" George asked.

"But we just had ice cream!" Nancy said.

"I only had one spoonful," George said.

"And I spit mine out," Bess said. "So that doesn't count."

The girls pedaled their bikes two blocks to River Street. As they parked them, they noticed a sign in the window of the Mean Bean Health Food Store. It read SMOOTHIES! 100% REAL FRUIT.

Nancy, Bess, and George walked inside. The store always smelled like the inside of a vitamin bottle.

"This is the place that Kevin's parents own," George whispered. "If he's here, maybe we can ask him questions."

"Sure," Nancy said. But deep inside she still didn't think Kevin stole Kendra's recipe.

Mr. Garcia stood behind the juice counter. He made three smoothies—strawberry for Bess, banana for George, and banana-strawberry for Nancy.

"Is Kevin here?" Bess asked.

Mrs. Garcia walked over from the vitamin shelf. "Kevin is out spending his birthday money," she said.

"Hopefully on that new Yoga for Kids DVD!" Mr. Garcia said with a grin. "I heard it really rocks!"

"Can we add some wheat grass juice to your smoothies?" Mrs. Garcia asked. "Very healthy!"

"And tasty!" Mr. Garcia added.

"Grass?" George gulped.

"Um . . . no, thank you," Nancy said.

The three friends carried their smoothies out of the store. They were about to stick their straws through the plastic lids when Kendra huffed over.

"Smoothies?" Kendra cried. "You're supposed to be finding out who stole my recipe. The contest is tomorrow!"

"We were having a high-energy snack," George

said. "So we'll have lots of strength to solve the case!"

But Nancy knew Kendra was right. Time was running out.

"We'll do our best, Kendra," Nancy promised.

Kendra heaved a big sigh. Then she ran to catch up with her mother.

"We *have* to solve this case, Clue Crew," Nancy said. "Let's sit down somewhere and really get to work!"

The girls saw a bench in front of the Chocolate Soldier Shop. As they walked toward it, the door of the shop swung open. A boy rushed out with a box tucked under his arm. On the box was a picture of a chocolate soldier.

"It's Kevin," Nancy whispered.

The girls ducked behind the bench. Between the wooden slats they watched Kevin running to a shiny blue bike parked at the curb. He dropped the box into the bike basket, then pulled on a helmet, climbed on, and pedaled away.

"That didn't look like a yoga DVD to me,"

George said. "He spent his birthday money on chocolate!"

"No one can eat that much chocolate," Bess asked. "Not even Kevin Garcia!"

"Unless he's not eating it," Nancy said slowly.

"What do you mean?" George asked.

"Maybe Kevin *did* enter the ice-cream contest," Nancy said slowly. "And maybe he *is* making Kendra's ice cream!"

ChaPTER EighT

Ice Scream!

"Let's follow Kevin on our bikes," Nancy suggested. "And see what he's up to."

"And lose our awesome fruit smoothies?" George asked. "Nuh-uh!"

The girls sat on the bench slurping their drinks.

"Maybe there's a way to find out if Kevin entered the ice-cream contest," Nancy said.

"The Jim and Barry Ice Cream Factory is on this street," George said. "Do you think the guys would let us see the sign-up list?"

"We can ask them," Nancy said.

The girls finished their smoothies. Then they rode their bikes all the way down the street to the Jim and Barry Ice Cream Factory. After filing through the revolving doors they looked around. The lobby wall was covered with pictures of Jim and Barry. A guard was sitting at a big wooden desk. Her nameplate read BEVERLY SHAW.

"We're not giving away ice cream, kids," Beverly said.

"We don't want any ice cream," Nancy said.

"We just want to see the sign-up list for the contest, please," George said.

"Sorry, girls," Beverly said. "That list is private."

"Then can we meet Jim and Barry?" Bess asked.

"Jim and Barry are hard at work," Beverly said, shaking her head. "They're coming up with the next flavor."

"What is it?" Nancy asked.

"That's private too," Beverly said. Her phone rang. She picked it up and said, "Jim and Barry's Ice Cream."

The girls traded glances as Beverly began talking. There had to be a way to get inside the factory and speak to Jim and Barry!

"Hold on, sir. I'll check the calendar," Beverly

said into the phone. She opened her desk drawer and began rummaging through it.

"Come on!" George hissed.

In a blink, the girls were tiptoeing quickly and quietly down the hallway. At the end of the hall was a big steel door. A sign on it read EMPLOYEES ONLY!

"What are em-ploy-ees?" Nancy asked.

"Maybe kids who signed up for the ice-cream contest!" George said with a smile. "Are we lucky or what?"

The girls pushed at the door until it swung open.

"Brr!" Bess said as they walked into the room. "It's freezing in here!"

The room was brightly lit and sparkling clean. It was filled with big steel vats. The vats were almost as tall as the girls.

"No wonder it's cold," Nancy said, rubbing her arms. "This must be where they make the ice cream!"

George ran over to a vat. She grabbed the rim and hoisted herself up. Then she peered into the

vat and said, "Wowie! I think this is my favorite—
Whooooaaaaaa!"

Nancy gasped. George was falling headfirst
into the vat! She and Bess grabbed George's feet
and held on tight.

"I like ice cream, but not this much!"
George shouted. "Heeeelp!"

"We're trying!" Nancy grunted. She and
Bess tugged on George's feet until they finally
pulled her out of the vat.

"Whew!" George said. "That was close!"

"No," a voice said. "That was Mint, Mint, Hooray!"

The girls whirled around. Jim and Barry were standing in the room.

Nancy stared at the guys. They wore white coats and hairnets over their hair.

"We're not giving tours yet, kids," Jim said.

"The door said . . . em-ploy-ees," George said. "That means—"

"People who work here," Barry explained with a grin. "You're a bit young for a factory job."

"And you shouldn't be here without a grown-up," Jim added.

"Sorry," Nancy said. "We just wanted to see the sign-up list for the ice-cream contest tomorrow."

"We're already on the list," George said. "But we want to see if someone from school is on it too."

"Can we?" Bess asked. "Please?"

"No can do," Jim said.

"But we can't wait to taste your ice cream tomorrow," Barry said brightly. "Just try not to fall into it!"

The guys held the door for Nancy, Bess, and George as they left the big, cold room.

"How neat was that?" Bess squealed. "We got to meet Jim and Barry—up close and personal!"

"But we didn't get to see the list." Nancy sighed. "And when the guard sees that we sneaked in—she's going to have kittens!"

As they neared the guard's desk, Nancy noticed something. There was a *different* guard at the desk this time. His nameplate read MATT STEVENSON.

"Brainstorm," George whispered.

Nancy and Bess followed George to the desk.

"Hi," George said. "We just want to make sure our names are spelled right on the contest list."

Matt reached into the top drawer of his desk and pulled out the sign-up sheet. "Here you go!" he said.

The girls huddled over the list. Bess jabbed her finger at one of the names: Kevin Garcia!

"Did you spell your names right?" Matt asked.

"Yes!" the girls said together.

"Then good luck in the contest tomorrow,"

Matt said. "And if you win, save a pint of ice cream for me!"

Nancy, Bess, and George zipped through the revolving doors. Once outside, they raced toward their bikes.

"Kevin *did* enter the contest," George said.

"We have to check Kevin out," Nancy said. "But I have no idea where he lives."

"Me neither," George said with a shrug.

"Two hundred Crescent Street!" Bess said. "It was right next to his name."

"How do you know?" Nancy asked.

"Not only can I build and fix things," Bess said proudly, "I have a great memory too!"

The girls pedaled the three blocks to Crescent Street. They found Kevin's house in the middle of the block. They stepped up to the door, and Nancy rang the doorbell over and over again. They walked to a window and peeked inside. The Garcias' housekeeper was busy vacuuming the living room.

Rrrrr! Rrrrr!

"No wonder she can't hear the doorbell,"

George said. "That vacuum cleaner sounds like a rocket booster!"

Nancy saw a path leading around the house to the backyard. "Let's check out the back," she said. "Kevin might be hanging out there."

"Or making ice cream!" Bess said with a frown.

The girls followed the path to the backyard. They didn't see Kevin, just some patio furniture and a small white toolshed.

Suddenly Nancy spotted something on the grass near the shed. It looked like a crumpled-up candy bar wrapper. She picked it up and flattened it out. It was a wrapper from the Chocolate Soldier Shop.

"That's where Kevin bought the chocolate," Nancy said.

"Maybe Kevin made the ice cream already," George said. "And he's stashing it in a freezer inside the shed."

Nancy wanted to look inside. She turned the handle on the shed door. The wooden door creaked as she pushed it open.

The girls filed inside the shed. They jumped as the door slammed shut. With only one tiny window, it was very dark in the shed!

"Let's go," George said. "I don't see any—"

"Oooooh!" a voice moaned.

Nancy froze.

"Oooooh!"

There it was again! Nancy felt Bess grab her arm.

"Wh-what was th-that?" Bess stammered. "A ghost?"

CHAPTER NINE

What's for Dessert?

"Ooooh—my stomach!" the voice moaned.

"That's not a ghost," Nancy said. "It's Kevin!"

George opened the door for light. Behind a pile of firewood the girls found Kevin. He was sitting on the floor, surrounded by crumpled candy bar wrappers, a chocolate drink can, and an empty Popsicle box!

"Aha!" George said. "Caught chocolate-handed!"

"What are you doing here?" Kevin groaned. His face was smudged with chocolate stains. So was his white T-shirt.

"We're looking for Chock Full of Chocolate ice cream," Bess said with a smirk. "Got any?"

"Chocolate!" Kevin groaned. He stuck out his

tongue and made a gagging sound. "Don't even say the word!"

Nancy felt bad that Kevin had a stomachache. But she was aching to ask him questions!

"What's the deal with all this chocolate,

Kevin?" Nancy asked. "You're not even allowed to eat it."

"That's why I spent my birthday money on tons of the stuff," Kevin explained. "My mom and dad said I could spend it on anything I wanted."

"So you ate it *all*?" Bess asked.

"Yeah. But don't remind me!" Kevin groaned again.

"Your name was on the contest list," George said. "Weren't you going to use the chocolate to make ice cream?"

"Some of it," Kevin admitted. "But I kept eating and eating and eating until nothing was left."

"I don't get it, Kevin," Nancy said. "Why did you enter a contest to win something you can't eat?"

"That's the idea!" Kevin said. "If I had that silver ticket, I'd be able to eat all the ice cream I wanted."

"Not if your parents have to sign a permission slip, too," Nancy pointed out.

Kevin stared at Nancy. Then he slapped his forehead with the back of his hand. "A permission slip?" he said. "Now you tell me!"

Nancy saw a Popsicle stick on the floor. As she kneeled down to pick it up, Kevin burped. His eyes bulged out as he covered his mouth with his hand.

"Back up! He's going to hurl!" George shouted.

The girls raced out of the shed. They were halfway through the yard when Nancy decided to run back.

"Kevin?" Nancy called through the door. "Are you okay?"

"Yeah," Kevin called back. "Just a dry heave."

Nancy, Bess, and George walked slowly back to their bikes.

"I guess Kevin is innocent," Bess said.

Nancy examined the Popsicle stick she took from the shed. "This doesn't say 'Lickety Sticks' on it," she said. "So Kevin did not write the message on my doorstep."

"Now we really have zero suspects." George sighed. "And the contest is tomorrow!"

Nancy suddenly heard bells. The Mr. Drippy truck was rolling down the street. It pulled up to the sidewalk and stopped.

The girls watched as a six-year-old boy made his way to the truck. He seemed to know the drill as he approached the window and saluted Mr. Drippy. "One vanilla ice-cream bar, please!" he said.

"At ease, young man," Mr. Drippy said.

While Mr. Drippy dug through the freezer, Nancy looked through the truck window. Henderson was standing in the back of the truck. He had two Popsicle sticks stuck up his nose and was snorting like a walrus!

"Gross!" Bess muttered.

Nancy was about to turn away from Henderson when something clicked. She ran over to the boy with the ice-cream bar and said, "Can we see that pop?" she asked.

"Sorry," the boy said. "You forgot to say—"

"Please!" Nancy groaned.

The boy looked confused as Nancy examined the Popsicle stick. "Bingo!" Nancy said. "This stick has 'Lickety Sticks Company' stamped on it!"

Nancy gave the ice-cream bar back to the boy. He walked away, shaking his head.

"Maybe Henderson wrote the Popsicle stick message, Nancy!" Bess said.

"Why would Henderson tell us to give up?" George asked. "He didn't enter the contest."

Nancy shrugged. "Maybe Henderson read about our case on Deirdre's Web site," she said. "And was just being pesty."

"Like always." Bess sighed.

It was two o'clock in the afternoon. George had promised to watch her baby brother while her mother planned the mayor's party. Bess's grandparents were visiting that afternoon, so she wanted to go home.

"That's okay," Nancy said with a smile. "I'll work on the case alone for a while."

Nancy knew it wouldn't be easy. Especially when the contest was tomorrow and she didn't have a clue.

"I don't know what to do, Daddy," Nancy said that evening. "Kendra wanted us to find the ice-cream thief in time for the contest tomorrow. And we blew it!"

Mr. Drew was busy chopping carrots for the dinner salad. "No, you didn't," he said. "Clues can show up anytime—even at the last minute."

Nancy smiled as her dad popped a carrot slice into her mouth. She swallowed and said, "I sure hope so, Daddy. Because this *is* the last minute!"

"Hi, George," Nancy said. "Are you ready for the contest?"

It was Saturday morning. Nancy and Bess

were standing on the Faynes' doorstep. In less than an hour the Jim and Barry Ice-Cream Flavor Contest would begin.

George waved Nancy and Bess inside. "I guess," she said. "But I'm bummed out about not solving the case."

"You're not the only one." Nancy sighed.

What would they tell Kendra when they saw her? And what would happen to the Clue Crew now? Would they be the big joke of River Heights Elementary School?

The girls walked into the kitchen. Mrs. Fayne was talking loudly on the phone.

"We didn't order orange carnations!" she said. "We ordered red roses! Red roses!"

"Mayor Strong's birthday party is today," George whispered. "My mom is so nervous she almost brushed her teeth with sunscreen this morning."

Nancy saw a big cardboard box on the kitchen table. "What are those?" she asked.

"Just the menus for the party," George said.

"Anything yummy on it?" Bess asked.

"If it's not a pizza party—who cares?" George said.

Bess picked up a menu and began to read out loud: "They're having something called Caesar Salad. The main course is salmon and asparagus. And for dessert there's . . . Chock Full of Chocolate Ice Cream."

Nancy blinked hard.

Say what?

"Bess!" she said. "Did you just say what I think you just said?"

CHAPTER TEN

Choco-Late!

"That's what it says," Bess said. "See for yourself!"

All three girls examined the menu.

"It *is* Chock Full of Chocolate Ice Cream!" Nancy said.

"*The* Chock Full of Chocolate Ice Cream?" George asked.

"It's got to be Kendra's recipe!" Nancy said. "But how did it land up on the menu for the mayor's party?"

"Mom!" George called. "How did you get Chock Full of Chocolate Ice Cream for the party?"

Mrs. Fayne was just hanging up the phone. "I didn't, George," she said. "Three gallons of it were delivered to Mayor Strong yesterday as a birthday present."

"By whom?" Nancy asked.

"I don't know," Mrs. Fayne said. "But I had to change the menu at the last minute."

The phone rang and Mrs. Fayne picked it up. "Hello?" she said. "No! I ordered *bagels*—not beagles!"

Nancy couldn't believe it. Her dad was right. Clues sometimes *did* pop up at the last minute!

"We have to go to the mayor's house," Nancy told Bess and George. "And find out who sent that ice cream."

Bess looked at her blue wristwatch. "But the ice-cream contest is in less than half an hour," she said. "We have to bring our Clue-berry ice cream to the factory!"

"We'll take it with us," Nancy said. "Come on!"

Bess grabbed the pint of Clue-berry from the Faynes' freezer. They rushed out of the house and ran the short distance to the mayor's house. On the way a voice yelled out, "Clue Crew! Wait up!"

Nancy glanced over her shoulder. It was Kendra, running right behind them!

"The ice-cream contest is today!" Kendra

shouted. "Did you solve the case? Well, did you?"

"We'll find out soon, Kendra!" Nancy shouted back.

The girls were out of breath when they reached the mayor's big yellow house. Nancy used the shiny brass knocker to rap on the door. The mayor himself answered the door. He smiled when he saw the girls.

"Happy birthday!" Nancy blurted. "Can you please tell us who gave you Chock Full of Chocolate ice cream?"

The mayor smiled. "Chock Full of Chocolate," he said. "You know, when I was a kid, chocolate was my favorite—"

"Please, Mayor Strong!" George cut in.

Mayor Strong's eyes widened. "All righty then," he said. "The ice cream was given to me by Chuck Murphy."

"Who's he?" Nancy asked.

"You kids know him as Mr. Drippy," Mayor Strong said. "Now I'd better get ready for my birthday party."

The girls stared at the door as it closed.

"Excuse me," Kendra said. "But how did that mean Mr. Drippy get my ice-cream recipe?"

As Nancy thought, she remembered Henderson.

"Henderson was at the factory on sign-up day," Nancy said. "Maybe he stole the recipe to give to his dad."

"Why would *he* steal my recipe?" Kendra asked.

A boy suddenly whizzed by on a skateboard. Nancy couldn't believe their luck. It was Henderson!

"Why don't we ask him?" Nancy said.

The four girls raced after Henderson.

"Henderson Drippy—I mean Murphy!" Nancy called. "We have to ask you something!"

Henderson looked back. He kicked and kicked to make his board go faster.

Nancy, Bess, George, and Kendra picked up speed. But they weren't quick enough for a speeding skateboard!

They were about to give up when another friend rattled down the block on roller skates. It was Deirdre Shannon!

Deirdre sped after Henderson. She caught

up to him and yelled, "Stoooooopppp!"

Henderson's board flipped out from under his feet. As he tried to catch it, Nancy, Bess, George, and Kendra raced over.

"I know what you want," Henderson said. "So I did write the message with the Popsicle sticks. Get over it!"

"We know you wrote the message," Nancy said. "But how did your dad get Chock Full of Chocolate ice cream?"

"What's the big deal?" Henderson asked. "I didn't want everyone buying Jim and Barry's ice cream instead of my dad's. So when I found this cool recipe for Chock Full of Chocolate, I gave it to him!"

"Did you say . . . found?" Kendra asked.

"Yeah," Henderson said. "It was on the ground."

Nancy turned slowly to Kendra. "Kendra," she said. "Your backpack doesn't have a hole in it . . . does it?"

Kendra took off her backpack. She touched the bottom of the front pocket and gulped. "Whoops," she said.

Nancy felt the slit under the pocket. It was wide enough for a small piece of paper to fall out.

"Sorry, you guys," Kendra said. She turned to Deirdre. "You're not going to write about this, will you?"

"Not if you don't want me to," Deirdre said.

"Chock Full of Chocolate is still your flavor, Kendra," Nancy said gently. "You can still enter the contest."

"The contest is in a few minutes," Kendra wailed. "I can't whip up a new batch of ice cream by then!"

"Oh, yeah?" Henderson said. "Watch this!"

Henderson put two fingers in his mouth and let out three sharp whistles. In a few seconds the Mr. Drippy truck rolled around the corner!

"Dad!" Henderson said as the truck stopped. "This is Kendra. She invented the Chock Full of Chocolate recipe."

The girls expected Mr. Drippy to glare at Kendra and insist that Chock Full of Chocolate was his recipe now. Instead Mr. Drippy smiled and said, "Good job, young lady!"

"Thanks," Kendra said. "But I don't have any to enter in the contest."

Mr. Drippy picked up a big cardboard box. On it was written "Chock Full of Chocolate." "Then you're going to need this!" he declared.

"My ice-cream flavor made into ice-cream pops!" Kendra exclaimed. "Cool!"

The girls raced around the corner to the Jim and Barry's Ice Cream Factory. Mr. Drippy's truck followed, his jingle blaring. At the factory, Nancy, Bess, George, and Kendra ran up onto the stage with their ice creams. Kendra smiled as she held a Chock Full of Chocolate ice-cream pop. Nancy was proud to hold their container of Clue-berry.

After another dance number by the tapping ice-cream cones, Jim and Barry stepped up to the microphone. They wore T-shirts with tuxedos printed on them.

"Let the contest begin!" Jim shouted.

Jim and Barry went down the line, tasting each flavor of ice cream. They liked the fan club's Oatmeal Raisin Cookie Crunch. They loved Kendra's Chock Full of Chocolate.

"It's our turn," Bess whispered as Jim and Barry walked over.

"And what's your ice cream called?" Jim asked.

"Clue-berry!" Nancy, Bess, and George said together.

"Snappy name," Barry said. "Let's have a taste."

Nancy smiled as she handed Barry the container. But when he pulled off the lid, the container tipped and—

Splat!

Nancy, Bess, and George gulped as they stared

at the puddle on the stage. Their Clue-berry ice cream had melted!

"Um," George said. "Can we enter a milk-shake?"

"Maybe next year," Jim said.

"But nice try, girls," Barry said.

As the guys walked to the next contestant, Nancy felt awful. But what did they expect after carrying their ice cream around in the hot sun for almost an hour?

In the end, the winner wasn't Kendra. Or the Jim and Barry Fan Club. To everyone's surprise, it was Kevin Garcia!

At the last minute Kevin came up with an entry called Naturally Nutty. It was made with frozen yogurt, dried apricots, and all kinds of nuts.

It was the perfect flavor for Jim and Barry. Especially since they wanted to sell a healthier new frozen dessert!

After the contest, Kevin waved his silver ticket in one hand. In the other hand was his parents' permission slip.

"My mom and dad said I can visit the factory once a month," Kevin explained. "So long as I pick a flavor they think is okay."

"What are you going to pick first?" Nancy asked.

"Anything but chocolate!" Kevin said, laughing.

Kendra ran over with a big smile. "Guess what?" she said. "Mr. Drippy is naming my ice cream after me. So every bar will say Kendra's Chock Full of Chocolate!"

"Way to go," Nancy cheered.

"You'll be as famous as Jim and Barry!" George said.

"I can't wait to write about this contest," Deirdre said. "Nancy, Bess, George? Can I call your ice cream Goo-berry?"

"*No!*" the three girls said together.

"Oh well." Deirdre sighed. "Come on, Kendra. Pose in front of the Mr. Drippy truck so I can take your picture."

Nancy was glad that Kendra and Deirdre were friends again. But she *was* sad that Clue-berry turned out to be a mushy mess. As they waited for Hannah to pick them up, Nancy, Bess, and George talked about the contest.

"We lost," Bess said sadly.

"Big-time!" George added.

Nancy turned to her two best friends and smiled.

"But we did solve the case, Clue Crew," she said. "And that makes us winning detectives!"

Nancy, Bess, and George's Coffee-Can Ice Cream

Nancy, Bess, and George know that making ice cream can be as easy as one, two, freeze! All you need is a sweet tooth and these simple ingredients:

1/2 cup milk
1/2 teaspoon vanilla
1 tablespoon sugar
4 cups crushed ice
4 tablespoons salt
Standard size coffee can with plastic lid
*Economy size (jumbo) coffee can with
   plastic lid.
A hand towel or gloves to keep fingers
   from freezing. Brr!

E-Z INSTRUCTIONS:

Mix the milk, vanilla, and sugar together in the smaller coffee can. Seal the can with the plastic lid. Put the can inside the larger can. Fill the larger can with ice and salt, and seal with the plastic lid. Now you have one can inside another!

READY TO ROLL!

Using your hand, roll the can back and forth on the ground until the ice cream is firm. Five to ten minutes is enough time for the mixture to freeze.

Now here comes the best part. . . . Grab a spoon, dig in, and enjoy!

FUN FACTOID

The ice-cream cone was invented at the St. Louis expo in 1904! The vendor ran out of plates and used rolled-up waffles instead! The rest is ice-cream history!

(*No jumbo coffee can at home? Try a restaurant or teacher's cafeteria for an empty one!)

13693